First

Dear Dean & April,
I wanted you to have this. You have been such a good friend to Kurt, and done so much for the Lord, and for our Church. God Bless you, and enjoy.
Love,
Joyce

a collection of intimate thoughts
from the heart of . . .

KURT HOLLEFREUND

© Copyright 2003 Kurt Hollefreund. All rights reserved.

No part of this publication may be reproduced, stored in a retrieval system, or transmitted, in any form or by any means, electronic, mechanical, photocopying, recording, or otherwise, without the written prior permission of the author.

Published in cooperation with Wobble City Press.

Printed in Victoria, Canada

Note for Librarians: a cataloguing record for this book that includes Dewey Classification and US Library of Congress numbers is available from the National Library of Canada. The complete cataloguing record can be obtained from the National Library's online database at: www.nlc-bnc.ca/amicus/index-e.html

ISBN 1-4120-0938-3

TRAFFORD

This book was published *on-demand* in cooperation with Trafford Publishing. On-demand publishing is a unique process and service of making a book available for retail sale to the public taking advantage of on-demand manufacturing and Internet marketing. **On-demand publishing** includes promotions, retail sales, manufacturing, order fulfilment, accounting and collecting royalties on behalf of the author.

Suite 6E, 2333 Government St., Victoria, B.C. V8T 4P4, CANADA
Phone   250-383-6864   Toll-free   1-888-232-4444 (Canada & US)
Fax   250-383-6804   E-mail   sales@trafford.com
Web site   www.trafford.com   TRAFFORD PUBLISHING IS A DIVISION OF TRAFFORD HOLDINGS LTD.
Trafford Catalogue #03-1307   www.trafford.com/robots/03-1307.html

10   9   8   7   6   5   4   3   2

in appreciation

It may sound strange coming from an 'author', but I find it difficult to put into words just how much the encouragement of friends has meant to me over the years. I have drawn strength repeatedly from your well of words. It is with the hope that through my writings, I am able to give back to you some of that same encouragement which you have so graciously given to me.

A special 'Thanks' goes to my friends John Selman and Nora Walker who freely offered their technical expertise. Once again you have demonstrated what friendship is all about!

I would also like to express my thanks to the staff at TRAFFORD PUBLISHING for their guidance and assistance in bringing this project to fruition.

Finally, I would be remiss if I did not give credit to my Heavenly Father for the many gifts that He has blessed me with, including special friends.

a note of explanation

My creative writing began later in life in response to a deep need of an old friend. Over time, as I expressed with pen and paper my responses to different situations that crossed my path, my collection grew. Publishing my writings was never my intention. Alas, I have caved in to peer pressure! You will be relieved to know that I have not included all of my writings!

While I have tried my best to protect privacy, it is also worth mentioning that not all selections were written for specific persons. I trust you will enjoy these thoughts as you read. Perhaps you might even find a ray of light in them that will help make your day just a little bit brighter. Thanks for reading!

Kurt Hollefreund

Contents

Humor:

I Am A Muller
Halloween Fun
Monday Morning Rise
The Coming Of Age
Medication For The Soul

Inspiration:

My Old Guitar
Freedom Remembered
The Value Of A Friend
The Forgotten Path To Freedom
Waiting In The Wings
Don't Let Go
Sonshine
The Winter Of Life

Contents

Spiritual:

The Lord, My Shepherd
Our Risen Hope
My Father's Love
Come Here My Child
Life's Journey
Thanksgiving
If Not For You. . .Then Who?
Mountain Mover
The Call
A Limo' Driver's Prayer
Morning Praise
My Valentine

Romantic:

A Touch Of Spring
Sweet Dreams
Sweetie
The Blanket Of Your Love
Through Princess Eyes

Contents

First Light . . .
Isn't It Amazing
My Friend . . . My Spouse
Commitment

Reflective:

Longings For Spring
Reflections Of My Heart
Simplicity
Courage
A Gift That Lasts
Halloween Confusion

Epilogue:

'So Long!

First Light...

Humour...

I Am A Muller
Halloween Fun
Monday Morning Rise
The Coming Of Age
Medication For The Soul

I AM A MULLER

I am a 'Muller', yes I am,
I think 'bout what you've said.
I let the words you give to me
Go 'round inside my head.

They tumble and they spin about
Back and forth again,
Until I've strained out every thought
You've shared in your refrain.

So please be patient as you wait
To hear what's in my head;
You see, I am a 'Muller',
And I think 'bout what you've said!

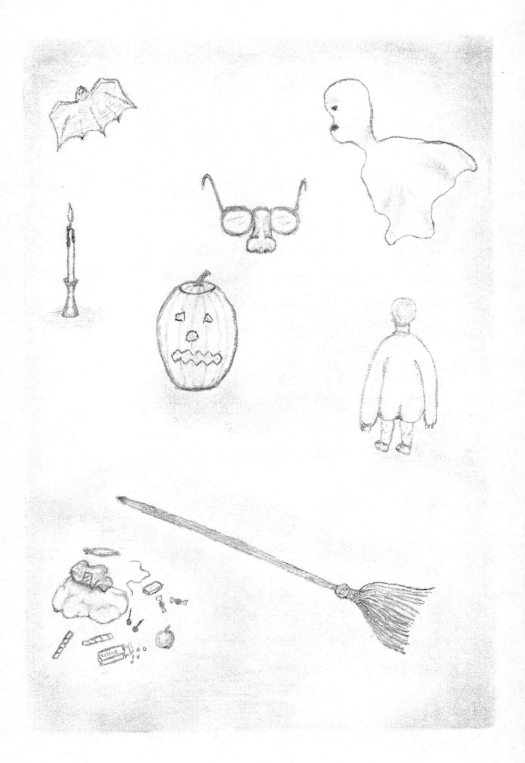

HALLOWEEN FUN

It was just moments
Before Halloween,
And as the telephone rang,
I heard a blood-curdling scream!
Torn between
Which direction to go,
I picked up the phone
And said, "Would you hold?"

Then bolting right out
And into the hall,
I discovered Dad
Now 'climbing the wall'.
It seems the kids' costumes
That used to fit well
Were now all disheveled,
Not looking too swell.

Now I'm not sure from whom
Came that blood-curdling yell.
Was it the kids or Dad?
It's not easy to tell.
All four looked like they
Were 'bout all done in
While Trick-or-Treating
Had yet to begin!

The dress-up party
We'd planned for that night,
Without costumes certainly
Wouldn't seem right.
With the older kids fighting
And the youngest now wet,
Dad looked up and asked,
"Are we having fun yet?"

At the sight of all this
I started to moan.
Then I thought, "Oh my goodness,
I've forgotten the phone!"
"NOBODY MOVES
AND NO ONE GETS HURT",
In a loud voice I yelled
And hoped it would work.

Off to the phone
I darted with speed,
Only to find
There was now no need!
I guess they decided
To cancel their call,
So with blood pressure rising,
I returned to the hall.

There they all sat,
The three boys and Dad!
No one had moved
And I thought, "Hmm---not bad!"
A wee bit of Mothers'
Choleric love
Seems to work well
When push comes to shove!

Well, a little twist here
And a little pull there
Made those costumes look great,
Like we'd bought them somewhere.
And the kids? Well they
Forgot 'bout their clothes
When friends with candy
Came by in droves.

Later that night,
The kids in their beds,
Each living the party
Again in their heads;
With wrappers all strewn
On the bedroom floor
And costumes limply
Hung on each door;

With a kiss and a hug
We exit each room.
(And with energies spent
It's not a moment too soon.)
And as we look at each other,
The evening now done,
We both think to ourselves,
"Now wasn't this fun?!"

MONDAY MORNING RISE

Well here it is, Monday again!
It's back to the usual grind.
I throw back the covers, hit the alarm,
And hear the crack of my spine!!
Instantly, reminiscent thoughts
Flood into my head
Of former times and younger life
As I try to get out of bed.

Maybe I'll just lay a while
And listen to the news:
"...The price went up on something else..."
(Yawn) "...the Premier bought new shoes..."
Wait a minute, you're drifting off,
Falling asleep again.
Suddenly a familiar voice
Reverberates my brain!

"Come on, get up! Open your eyes!
Wiggle your little toes."
"Oh leave me alone, my eyes are open,
Only the lids are closed!
I am awake (inside of me)
And why do you have to yell?
So loud, so early in the morn,
I'm moving, can't you tell?"

Oh well, all right. Now sit up straight.
Put your feet on the floor.
Lift your arms, crack your bones,
And try to reach the door!
Easy now, don't stub your toe,
And watch out for that chair!!
Into the bathroom safe at last,
Now, shave and comb your hair.

And don't forget to wash your face
Like you did the other day.
Well, so what if I missed one wash,
Who cares anyway?
Come on now, it's time to go.
You're gonna be late for work.
(Sigh) Well I guess that I had better move
But why does it always hurt?

I hate to face the ugly thought
That I am growing old,
But that's something I can't avoid,
At least that's what I'm told.
I twist and turn and exercise
To get me into shape,
And when I'm done they tell me that
I really will feel great.

But I don't know, it seams to hurt
More and more each day.
No matter what I try and do,
It still ends ups the same.
Some things in life are really tough
And fill us full of sighs,
But for me, there's nothing quite as rough
As the MONDAY MORNING RISE!!

THE COMING OF AGE

While I was walking down the street
Just the other day,
This little guy came scooting past
As I heard him say,
"Hey Old Man, quick step aside,
You're standing in my way."
Then, just as fast as he'd appeared,
He began to fade.

Hmm. . .I thought. 'Old Man', he said.
What gave my age away?
Was it that I walked too slow?
Or thinning hair of gray?
Maybe it is how I talk
With words I choose to say.
I'm not quite sure but still I yelled,
"You have a real nice day!"

I never thought myself as 'Old'
No matter what my age;
Always felt so young inside
All throughout my days.
Am I now 'Over the Hill'?
Will my mind now stray?
I wondered if senility
Would soon appear and stay.

Well, I hadn't gone too far
When, feeling sort of shunned,
An 'Old Man' with a cane called out
And said, "Please help me Son."
The light had changed to 'DON'T WALK' now
So he had tried to run.
I laughed and helped him cross the street
And thought, Boy, this is dumb!

Here I was, caught in time,
While 'Old' to that small one,
Moments later, down the block,
This 'Old Guy' thinks I'm young!
It's no surprise I get mixed up
And feel like I'm all done. . .
Don't know if I'm still in my prime
Or if my 'spring has sprung!'

Kind of leaves me hanging there
'Tween past and years to come.
Makes me feel unsure and all. . .
Like my mind's been spun.
Perhaps it's not too good to think
'Bout years that have been rung.
But rather, with the time that's left,
Just try to have some fun!

MEDICATION FOR THE SOUL

As I sit in contemplation
Of your present situation,
I offer medication
For your soul.

To experience such affliction
As ones' healthful restriction
Creates such a constriction
On the home.

When the kids start insurrection
And the house sees dereliction,
Yes, you've lost your days' direction
Down a hole,

Reach down through your frustration
While by-passing degradation,
And let the aggravation
'Round you go!

Let your humouration
Rule your heart with jubilation;
May it bring a fresh elation
To your soul.

And know that my affection
Is heaped in your direction
Just to help make the correction
On your stroll!

Inspiration...

My Old Guitar
Freedom Remembered
The Value Of A Friend
The Forgotten Path To
    Freedom
Waiting In The Wings
Don't Let Go
Sonshine
The Winter Of Life

MY OLD GUITAR

While rummaging a while ago
Underneath the stairs,
I saw something that caught my eye
Buried back in there.
With interest sparked, I pursued
Past boxes, bags and stuff;
Pushing aside past memories
Forgotten under dust.

I stretched until within my grasp,
Suspended on a nail,
Hung my very first guitar,
Now looking worn and frail.
I hauled it out and held it up
To view it in the light. . .
Neglect and years of rough abuse
Now made it quite a sight!

Dents and cracks and chips galore. . .
It didn't look like much.
Still, I thought, I could restore it
With a loving touch.
Stains and stickers from the past
Had covered up the wood;
Broken pegs and missing strings. . .
I wondered if I should?

But then I thought of what this friend
For years had given me. . .
A means of heart's expression
And sweet serenity!
It's been a while since '58
When I first heard it's sound.
How could I now toss it away
And let my 'old friend' down?

Out came the tools that I would need
To grant my friend's repair.
And coupled with envisioned plans,
I set aside despair.
I stripped the ugly stains away
And sanded down the top,
But when two cracks came into view
I simply had to stop.

The cracks had caused to top to cave,
New bracing it would need.
So underneath, support I gave,
Inside where it's unseen.
Then, on I went about the task
Of blending out the marks
That over time neglectful use
Had left on every part.

I turned it over to continue
On the other side,
And with each stroke of sandpaper
I felt a swelling pride!
"This is good" I told myself,
"I see improvement.
I think investing in my friend
Is really time well spent."

So I continued skillfully,
Attentive to the task.
Impassioned pride now driving me,
The hours quickly passed.
From the body, now I moved
Up the weathered neck. . .
Broken pegs; missing strings;
Worn and dented frets.

I surveyed, rubbed and sanded
'Til my hands were sore,
But when I turned it over
I could see it needed more!
A little here; a little there;
I could hardly wait,
So on I pressed with diligence
And slowly it took shape.

With all the scars and marks now gone,
The bare wood looking fine,
My thoughts soon turned to colouring
This old guitar of mine.
No ordinary colour would
Suffice for my 'old friend',
But rather something special that
Would bring a radiant end!

I searched for many days until
The perfect choice I found,
But with the sample firm in hand
The stain was not around.
Bewildered, I approached the clerk
And asked what I could do.
She said, "It is a special stain
And must be mixed for you."

Ah yes, of course! What else would do
For this 'old friend' of mine?
Something 'Special', yes indeed
To clothe it's curves and lines.
And then, to seal the colour in,
A coating to protect. . .
She put before me something new
And said, "It is the best!"

Hurriedly I paid the price
And ran out to the car,
Quite anxious to arrive back home
And 'dress up' my guitar.
Although the stain was beautiful,
The process took a 'knack'.
And so I set aside some time
To plan out my attack!

With the back I would begin,
And then along the side;
Back and forth methodically
My brush would gently glide.
Flip it over; do the top,
Proceeding up the neck;
Then after fully staining all,
I'd give it time to set.

With colour fast, it was now time
To lock its beauty in.
So, brush in hand, I began
To seal its radiant end.
So beautiful, yet of no use,
No music could it bring,
For still it lacked the tuning pegs,
A bridge and all the strings.

Once again I ventured out
Down to the music store
To ask the clerk for all the parts
I needed for my chore.
With pegs fastened tightly on
And strings now all in place,
I closed my eyes; strummed my friend;
But oh! What a disgrace!

From such a lovely piece of work
Nice music I assumed,
But then of course, foolish me,
The strings were not in tune!
Finally, with work all done,
Each step with loving care,
I stood it up against the wall
And leaned back in my chair.

Yes indeed! So beautiful!
A lovely work of art!
Then suddenly a vagrant thought
Pierced straight through to my heart.
I took this old guitar that had
Been missing out of sight,
Invested money, time and love,
And brought it back to life.

Although it's just an instrument,
I ventured anyway.
Yet it is not unlike the folks
I pass by every day!
Souls that have been battered by
Life's merciless abuse.
Ones I'd given up hope on
Because they have no use.

Cracked and chipped with damaged hearts
They've hurt for oh so long,
Stuffed away with memories. . .
Alive, yet without song.
A loving touch is all they need
From someone who would care;
To freely gift their gift of love
And some compassion share.

To brush off life's gathered dust
And share with them some light;
To recognize their valued worth
And help them back to life.
To be that inner strong support
That mends the cracks of time;
A ray of hope to light their way
'Til they begin to shine.

Someone to smooth out jagged chips
Of bitterness and wrath;
To help remove unwanted stains
Absorbed along life's path.
To be, as if, a tuning peg
Attached to their heart's string;
To show them how to tune whatever
Discord life may bring.

Some are always bitter and
They hurt from deep within.
They've been hurt so many times
They're scared to love again.
Some are philosophical,
Lost in a 'state of mind'.
Not quite sure what they should do,
Just thinking all the time.

And then there are the bubbly ones,
Laughing all the while,
Trying to protect themselves
By hiding 'neath a smile.
I need to hold them in my arms
When they have seen such hurt
And look beyond their stains and scars
And see their valued worth.

To seal a life with love's strong bond
And hear its' music soar,
It is reward within itself,
How could I want for more?
So there it stands, my old guitar,
Restored as best I can,
To serve as a reminder
Of my fallen, fellow man.

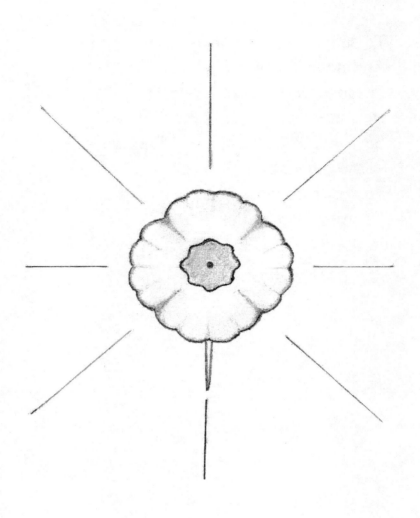

FREEDOM REMEMBERED

I seem to get some funny looks
While walking on the street.
I see them stare. . .then look away,
They try to be discreet.
One cannot blame them I suppose,
It is the month of June
And I still wear my 'Poppy'!
Am I late or just too soon?

You see, I struggle with some things
While going through my day.
My memory is one of them
As it begins to fade.
There was a time when in my life
My thinking was still keen,
But let me take a moment now
To share just what I mean.

I know the feeling that I get
While driving down the street.
At ease, I freely pick the place
Where I would like to eat.
With Bible tucked under my arm,
Each week I head to Church
With not a twinge of worry
'Bout what that freedom's worth.

Each day I take my car to work
And go about my job.
That freedom's driven home to me
Each time the jobless sob.
And I enjoy the privilege
When it comes time to vote,
Even if those in the race
Seem like a 'living joke'!

I've never had to leave my home
And march off to some war.
I am so very thankful for
The freedom from that chore!
Now all these things remain quite clear,
Reminders in my mind
Of luxuries I now enjoy
Paid for back in time.

But here's the part that bothers me,
And in this short refrain,
I will try just one more time
To sort it out again.
Each year we take one single day,
(It happens in the Fall)
And gather 'round to recognize
Our Vet'rans standing tall.

In uniform they look so sharp
'Til one begins to cry;
His thoughts have drifted off somewhere
To comrades he watched die.
We justify this one lone day
With Poppies we have bought,
Yet I can't seem to get it straight. . .
Which day was it they fought?

THE VALUE OF A FRIEND

The tailor sews the finest clothes
To fashion what he would.
We know he's done the best he can...
They look and feel so good.
The musician's fingers move so swift
And dance upon the keys.
The sounds and melodies he plays
Puts all of us at ease.

These artists do their very best
By practicing their skill,
Improving every stitch and note
According to their will.
'Just one more time' their motto is,
Re-doing with their hands.
Patience flows abundant as
Perfection this demands.

But what about the things in life
Not crafted by our hands?
The skills that come from in oneself,
Out from the heart of Man?
How do we see these varied skills
And gauge their final end?
The evidence is richly found
In commitment of a friend!

To have a friend that you can trust
To talk with night or day,
To share both good and bad times with
Along life's bumpy way.
To tell a joke, share a tale,
Sit with through the night,
In confidentiality
Disclose that inner fright.

Someone who will stick by you
Even through the bitter end,
I ask what standard can we use
To measure this true friend?
It's hard to do, no matter if
The friend is young or old,
For truest friends are priceless,
Worth more than purest gold!

Of all the skills found in our lives
Perfected by each man,
The greatest I would have to say
Is not performed by hand.
It is the skill of Character
That makes a person shine
And helps him do the things he does
To keep his life in line.

Some in life refine this skill
While others let it slide.
They think it unimportant so
They're 'just here for the ride'.
Not so with you, you've proved in life
On you we can depend.
So with respect, I've penned these words
For you my. . .'Special Friend'.

THE FORGOTTEN PATH TO FREEDOM

Ouch!! What is that piercing pain
Deep within my back?
Ah yes, now I know,
Another knife attack!
It seems so strange a thing to me
That we should have this need
To hurt and stab each others' back
Delighting in the deed.
What does one do to keep himself
Untainted in his mind
When it appears that all around
Respect has gone with time?

Disappeared...vaporized...
Vanished with the past...
A tragic situation left,
How long will this scene last?
Each defending his own thoughts
And actions he has done,
But when we reach the long days' end,
Has anybody won?
I think not; it's a facade;
A smoke screen at its' best;
And each and every one of us
Has failed a crucial test!

In each mans' heart, let's take a stand
To mend our damaged ways.
Instead of tearing others down,
How 'bout a little praise?
Find that part within a life,
Although it may be small,
And magnify it with respect
To make that life feel tall!
Do for them what you'd prefer
Done unto yourself,
And on our jobs and in our hearts,
Peace will be our wealth.

WAITING IN THE WINGS

I have a friend that I know,
A friend that's out of touch.
Her burdens weigh her down so low
She doesn't feel like much.

She's focused on her daily plight
While trudging through her day,
And missing little joys of life
Sent along her way.

The joy of nurturing a child
Whose trust is so complete;
The love of her adoring man
That's laid before her feet.

The flowers that are spread so free
All across the earth,
Their purpose? Just for her to see,
For which she never worked.

Friends that love her deeply
That would stand through thick or thin;
Ones that would uphold her
If she would allow them in.

I cannot force myself upon
This friend consumed with pain,
For her heart's door on which I knock
Must open from within!

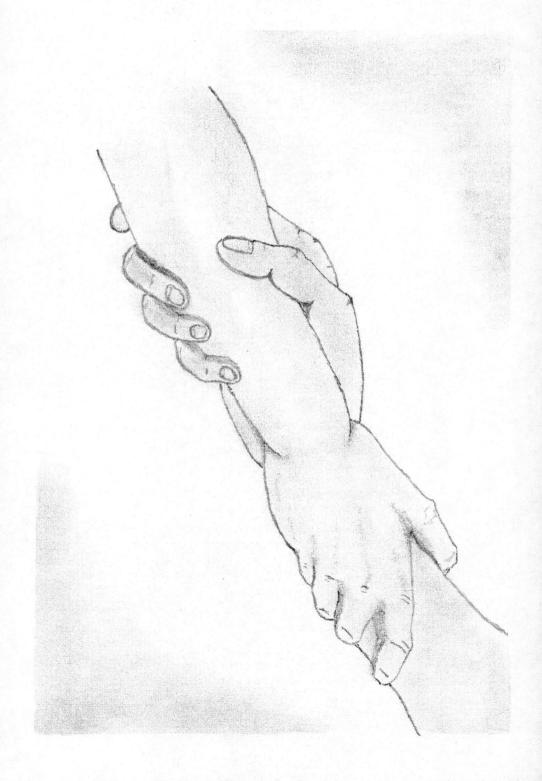

DON'T LET GO

The clouds of life came blowing in,
The wind began to scream;
And as I viewed my circumstance,
My faith began to wean.
I tried to grasp what'ere I could
To keep myself afloat,
But being tossed both to and fro'
My life still felt remote.

With apprehension surging caused
By trouble all around,
And conflict tearing at my life
I feared that I might drown!
In desperation I looked up
To the God I know
And begged Him, Please! To hold on tight!
He said, "Don't _you_ let go!

I've been holding all along,
You've had no need to fear.
For even through the storms of life
I've always been right here.
But through it all there is one thing
You need, to help you grow:
That's even though _I'm_ holding on,
You need to not let go!"

SONSHINE

Today, I viewed a lifeless form. . .
Crushed by the overpowering bite of grief!
A form left limp and void of desire. . .
Overshadowed by defeat.
Today, through a heavy heart,
I viewed You.

Yet, I see a stirring, a movement. . .sunshine.
Through the window of hope,
Bound by the frame of time,
I see a rustling.
Beneath the fallen leaves of days gone by
I see a resurrection to the warm rays of
Renewed life.

Take hold of this vision, for it is your
Tomorrow. Do not let it go!
Bask in its' warmth!
Allow its' touch to reach down deep
And soothe your wounded soul.
For it is in these rays of time to come that
You will receive new strength, new life. . .
Your victory!

Take time to live; take time to heal;
Take time to yield to the source
Of your renewed life.
His rays of love will sustain you,
For He is the Son!

THE WINTER OF LIFE

Weakly, it drew its' last drop of life.
Then, in a moment, it's
Calculated time had come.
Suddenly, ripped from its' home and
Driven by merciless gusts of wind,
It is forced to the ground.
Faded, dry and discoloured,
Its' life is now spent.

And as the bleakness of Winter sets in,
It remains. . .so very still.
Engulfed by the piercing ambiance of cold,
It is forgotten all too soon;
Passed over by the hustle and bustle of life;
Silently buried under the compounded layers
Of daily snowfalls.

And so is the season of Man.
Birthed and flourished within the
Confines of his surroundings,
With his life exhausted,
He falls to the ground;
Only to be covered up by the
Stark, cold layers of continued routine.

Forgotten under the blanket of
Daily agenda, he remains. . .
Until the rejuvenating rays
Of the Eternal Son
Melts away the coldness of time forgotten,
Resurrecting his form
In the Springtime of new life.

As a living gift bestowed upon him
By the Author of life,
He never again will be forgotten;
Forever to remain
A living, radiant, exhibition
Of the glorious righteousness
Of his Omnipotent Creator.

Spiritual...

The Lord, My Shepherd
Our Risen Hope
My Father's Love
Come Here My Child
Life's Journey
Thanksgiving
If Not For You...Then Who?
Mountain Mover
The Call
A Limo' Driver's Prayer
Morning Praise
My Valentine

THE LORD, MY SHEPHERD

Oh LORD, You are the One who oversees
Every detail of my life. You watch out for
Me; I have nothing to worry about!

Your presence makes my spirit content.
When life's journey makes me weary,
You lead me through times of bountiful
Refreshment.

You teach me how to walk through life the
Way I should, so I can be more like You.

Even though the circumstances surrounding
My life may be in turmoil, I will not be
Anxious or afraid for You are always right
Here with me.

Your correction and guidance are comforting
To me for I know they are designed for my
Well being.

When it seems that all are against me
And trouble surrounds me on every side,
In the midst of it all, You abundantly provide
For my needs of nourishment.

Your refreshing Holy Spirit pours over me,
Invigorating me to press on. Your blessings
Are more than I can contain.

Because of Your encompassing and unfailing
Love for me, I will bask in Your goodness and
Mercy the rest of my life.

With my heart as Your permanent home,
I will enjoy Your presence for all Eternity!

OUR RISEN HOPE

The sun broke through that early morn',
Yet, still the faces looked forlorn.
What a weekend this had been,
One like we had never seen!
Trouble from the pit of Hell
Had ruled this town in which we dwell.
Did this really happen here?
All we felt was chilling fear.

Priests had taken the Son of God,
Accused Him, mocked Him, had Him flogged.
Then, they nailed Him to a cross!
Oh my God, what a loss!
There He'd hung until He died. . .
All we could do was watch and cry. . .
All our hopes were based on Him,
And now. . .He's dead! Were we sucked in?

Had we been fooled by some slick plan?
Was He Messiah? Or merely man?
Not knowing just what we should do,
We felt it best to think things through.
And so we left to go our way,
Unsure of what would fill the day.
Suddenly, breaking through the gloom,
A radiant light burst from the tomb.

The ground below began to shake
As we endured a strong earthquake.
The heavy rock, so hard and cold,
That covered up the entrance hole,
Was being pushed off to the right
By someone dressed in glistening white.
The guards put there to keep it sound
Were lying crumpled on the ground.

Then the one with clothes that shone
Said, "Come and see that He is gone!
Jesus, who you know was dead,
Arose this morn' just like He said.
Quickly now, go back to town
And tell your friends what you have found."
With feelings mixed of fear and glee
We headed off excitedly,

Planning all along the way
The words of joy we had to say.
It felt as if we'd run a mile
When. . .there He stood. . .with His big smile,
Stopped us quick, right in our tracks!
He greeted us and said, "Relax!
Don't be afraid, I'm in control,
And I have now redeemed your soul.

I fought the fight, the battle's done;
I overcame and I have won!
The price is paid, my work's complete
And Satan lies in full defeat!
As you can see, I am alive!
Did you forget that I would rise?
Go tell our friends the news of me,
That I'll meet them in Galilee.

Instruct them to obey my word,
In faith applying what they've heard.
The power that has raised up me
Will transform you, you will see.
And I will always be with you
Providing strength for all you do.
So walk with me, your hand in mine,
From now until the end of time."

MY FATHER'S LOVE

I came before the LORD today
In clutches of withdraw'l.
I didn't quite know what to say,
My spirit felt so small.
Not understanding why it was
I felt so incomplete,
He lovingly admonished me,
"I need to wash your feet."

The dust and dirt that clung to me,
Picked up throughout my day,
Had somehow now misguided me
Causing me to stray.
I'd tried so many other things
In search of inner peace,
Yet, once again, He beckoned me,
"Please. . .Let me wash your feet!"

Why is it that I hesitate
When in my heart I know,
That nothing else will satisfy,
There's nowhere else to go!
I need to come before His throne
And in His presence sweet,
Humbly sit; just me. . .alone,
And let Him wash my feet!

COME HERE MY CHILD

Jesus says, "Come here my child,
Come and sit with me awhile.
I said that I'd take care of you.
Do you believe my words are true?
Did I not promise joy untold
If you'd let me have control?
The peace that comes from deep within,
You know it must with me begin.

I love you now, just as before,
And I will love you evermore.
Do not fret at what takes place
But look steadfastly on my face.
I am your strength, so lean on me;
I can uphold you, you will see.
I see your pain, your hurt and tears;
I'll not ignore your fragile fears.

Just come to me with all you have;
I'll give to you my precious salve.
A healing I will grant to you
From all the hurt that you've gone through.
As you from day to day now live,
Draw from me the strength I give.
I offer it with love from me:
I paid the price. . .for you it's free!"

LIFE'S JOURNEY

LORD, help me as I walk through life
To do the best I can.
Remind me while I take each step
To not judge fellow man.

And as I travel down life's road
With great expectancy,
Oh LORD, I humbly recognize
I'm here through sovereignty.

It's by your grace alone that I
Can rise to greet each day;
It's for your strength, that I now ask,
To follow in your way.

Be my light and constant guide
While traveling this road,
Until the day you call me home
To live in your abode.

THANKSGIVING

LORD, I want to thank you for
A life set free from sin.
You've opened up my heart and poured
Forgiveness deep within.

But <u>how</u> can I say 'Thanks' for
All the things that you have done:
For cleansing me. . .accepting me. . .
For making me your son?

Father, with a grateful heart,
The least that I can do,
Is offer up my life as 'Thanks'
And give it back to you!

IF NOT FOR YOU. . .THEN WHO?

While thinking 'bout my life today,
Of things that I have done,
I wonder what a tangled web
Unwittingly I've spun.
Events that bridge from joy to pain
Comprising what I do,
I ask, What is the purpose, LORD,
If not for You. . .then who?

The job that I attend each day;
The way I do my work;
And how each week I spend my cheque
To pay my way on earth;
The folks I meet and share life with
While living as I do;
What does it mean, oh LORD I pray,
If not for You. . .then who?

To share but one encouraging word
Or give a smile each day;
To help the friend who feels so low
Who's fallen on their way;
To give a lift to help that one
Their troubled day get through;
While placed upon this earth, oh LORD,
If not for You. . .then who?

To pass on wealth that's granted me,
The wealth I don't deserve;
To share the love You give so free
Your children to preserve:
Oh LORD, as I continue on
With life still left in view,
You are my only purpose so
I'll give my all for You!

MOUNTAIN MOVER

Father, You have said to come
To You with all our needs.
So, once again, I find myself
Here upon my knees.
There are so many mountains that
Seem to block my path,
Blotting out the rays of Hope
In which I like to bask.

There is the mountain, large in size,
The mount that's known as Doubt.
It sits and blocks my way today
And keeps your Sonshine out.
The next one's called Apathy,
And when I'm asked to share,
It hinders what I need to do
By saying "...no one cares!"

Another one that's in my way
Is Discouragement.
So ominous, it leaves me feeling
Insignificant!
But Father, it is not their size
That I will focus on,
For You're the 'Mountain Mover'
That I rely upon!

THE CALL

LORD, You've called me to go out
And take to other lands
The precious message of Your love
I carry in my hands.

To travel far, to travel wide,
To cover all the earth;
To let man know about Your love
And what it's really worth.

To share with those less fortunate
The gift of Your sweet Grace;
To give them Hope until the day
We see You face to face.

Come be my Guide as on my way
I travel foreign ground,
And be my Shield against the foes
That try to strike me down.

Use Your Strength to open doors
That are now fortified;
Doors, as yet I have not seen,
Appointed by Your eye.

Prepare the hearts of those that hear;
Provide for all my needs,
Until that day when I shall stand
With You eternally.

A LIMO' DRIVER'S PRAYER

LORD, be the 'Limo' of my life
In which I daily ride,
So as I travel on life's streets,
I can drive with pride.
Let Your love be the power
Underneath the hood;
Help me as I learn the rules
To drive just as I should.

May the joy that comes from You
Light my darkened way,
Keeping me upon the path
That's safe with You each day.
Allow the washing of Your Word
To keep the windshield clear
So I can see the obstacles
As they draw quickly near.

And as I follow in Your path
I pray, throughout the night,
The righteous acts that have been done
Would serve as bright tail lights
To send a message to the ones
Behind, so they would know,
That You're the 'Limo' of my life
And follow down the road.

MORNING PRAISE

Oh LORD, great are Your works
And how majestic is Your Name!

The dawn of my morning
Arrives by Your command.
The crispness of the new day comes
As a direct result of Your beckoning.
As the wispy vapours of my breath
Escape my being,
So I am reminded that they are
Your gift to me this day!

It is by Your Grace and Majestic Authority
That I, as Your child,
Have been granted yet
One more day to serve You.
I present my life before You today
In humble submission as
My offering of appreciation
For Your abiding love for me.

Oh LORD, great are Your works
And how majestic is Your Name!

MY VALENTINE

I loved you when I thought of you
Long before your birth;
I loved you at the moment when
You entered life on earth.

I loved you when, while trembling,
You first went off to school;
I loved you as the kids stood 'round
And mocked you like a fool.

I loved you when you knelt in prayer
And asked Me in your heart;
I loved you when you smiled and said,
"You'd never let us part!"

I loved you when you took a stand
For what you knew was right;
I loved you as your friends all left,
You stood alone that night.

I loved you when your spouse walked out,
They said they had to part.
I loved when you reached out to Me
To mend your broken heart.

I love when, as you start each day,
I'm kept in your hearts' eye;
And I'll love you forever Child,
For you are why I died!

    All my love,
                    ...Jesus

Romantic...

A Touch Of Spring
Sweet Dreams
The Blanket Of Your Love
Sweetie
Through Princess Eyes
First Light...
Isn't It Amazing
My Friend...My Spouse
Commitment

A TOUCH OF SPRING

Although it's only August I
See leaves now turning brown,
And as I look all 'round about,
They're falling to the ground.

With winters' entrance evident,
So cold and still and dark,
I'd like to thank you for the gift
Of 'Springtime' in my heart!

As you know, with shift work
Things don't always coincide:
Days are nights; nights are days;
And weekends seem to slide.

So I'll not fret, when in my life,
'Seasons' don't agree,
I'll just enjoy the freshness of
My 'Spring' when you're with me!

SWEET DREAMS

I wish I may,
I wish I might,
I wish that you
Were here tonight!

To sit and cuddle
In your arms;
To smell your hair
And feel your charms;

To have you here
All to myself,
Content for you
To be my wealth!

Alas, it wasn't
Meant to be,
So I'll just sit
And dream of thee!

THE BLANKET OF YOUR LOVE

Though the brisk November winds
Bring Winter's chill,
And skies are covered with
Rolling clouds of gray;

Though the trees grow bare
As they give way to Autumn's closing grip,
My heart rests cozy as it cuddles
Under the warm blanket of your love.

SWEETIE

Twinkle, twinkle, little Star.
Oh, how wonderful you are!
A little dimple on your face;
A smile that brightens up our place.

Toes and fingers all intact---
Your little body, so exact!
Eyes that sparkle with delight
As you absorb your brand new life.

A gift entrusted from above,
Sent to us on wings of love.
A living Gem for us to hold,
To teach and guide as you grow old.

And as you join our family,
You will be known as my 'Sweetie',
For nothing tastes as sweet as love
And that is you, my Precious Dove!

All my love,
Dad

THROUGH PRINCESS EYES

I'm so thankful for someone
Such as the likes of you,
One who always sees life's sights
With a compassionate view.

Thanks for noticing this 'frog',
Tho' times I make you sigh.
Yet you always look at me
Through precious 'Princess Eyes'.

Thanks for looking past the 'warts'
That cover my outside;
For treating me like you are proud
To have me by your side.

And thanks for all the things you do
Designed to meet my needs.
You're precious, and you need to know
My 'tadpole' heart is pleased.

FIRST LIGHT . . .

Haltingly, they flutter. . .
As I awake to absorb morning's
First light.

Instantly, I am flooded
With an awareness of my Creator's
Love for me.
His encompassing presence,
His watchful eye,
His forgiving grace. . .
I turn to view His gift of extravagance
. . .And You are there!

Lying still, cradled in the peaceful
Envelope of sleep,
You are my 'Eve'.
Precious, perfect and delectable;
A living token
Of my Father's love,
Uniquely gifted to meet my needs
Of relational completeness.
You are most cherished!

Haltingly, they flutter. . .
As you awake to absorb morning's
First light.

ISN'T IT AMAZING!!

Isn't it amazing. . .the miracle of birth!
The anticipated entrance
Of your life upon this earth;
Expected to survive
When you don't even know your worth.
I marvel at it all. . .isn't it amazing!

And isn't it amazing. . .growing up and all!
The problems that came 'cross our path
That seemed both great and small;
They somehow seemed so solvable
By shopping at the mall.
I chuckle at the thought. . .isn't it amazing!

Isn't it amazing. . .developing yourself!
Absorbing all the thoughts that will
Give intellectual wealth;
And learning how to keep yourself
In satisfactory health.
Ah. . .self development. . .isn't it amazing!

Yes, isn't it amazing. . .to have
One Special friend!
Someone with whom there is no doubt
Your life you want to spend;
To have that love from both of you
Now bind you 'til the end.
Oh, the power of love. . .isn't it amazing!

Isn't it amazing. . .two, born at
Diff'rent times,
Who have come from diff'rent cities and
From diff'rent family lines,
To filter out all of the rest
And just each other find.
What a coincidence. . .isn't God amazing!

MY FRIEND. . .MY SPOUSE

What a privilege it is
To have a 'Special Friend'.
One with whom to share your thoughts
And precious time to spend.
Discovering, as on you go,
That this friend means much more
Than all the other friends that passed
Through your life's open door.

And as time goes, to suddenly,
Come to realize
That this one very 'Special Friend'
Is now a treasured prize!
I think the ultimate would be
To take that 'Special Friend'
And love them just for who they are
And with them your life spend.

Surrendering each part of you
In open honesty;
In everything you say or do
Share that love so free.
Let that love, in 'Silver Boxes',
That you daily share,
Be continual reminders
Of commitment that is there.

Love is patient and so kind;
Is not envious;
It does not brag, nor is it proud;
It does not make a fuss.
It is not rude or selfish and
Is steadfast for so long;
Is not angered easily;
Does not record the wrongs.

In evil it does not delight;
Is joyful with the truth;
Always protects, trusts and hopes:
Endurance is the proof!
Cherish well your Friend, your Spouse;
Respect their gifts of love,
And you will know the happiness
You're both deserving of!

COMMITMENT

Well, what a year this has been
'Tween life and death and everything!
Confusing times and times of peace;
Restraints of life and sweet release.
Touching bounds of each extreme---
Sometimes it makes me want to scream!
So what is left that still holds true?
I guess one of those things is You!

I'm reassured as out I've looked
To see the both of you still 'hooked'.
I lean on your example set
As older and deeper in marriage I get.
I'm thankful for the two of you
And count on your commitment too.
You've become a ref'rence point
For us here in our humble joint.

To know that you have stuck it out
Encourages me, removing doubts.
Selfish? Yes, I suppose I am,
But I draw strength from where I can.
So yes, I guess my guilt is plain,
But I love you both all the same
And give my 'thanks' to each of you
For rev'rencing the words 'I Do'.

Reflective...

Longings For Spring
Reflections Of My Heart
Simplicity
Courage
A Gift That Lasts
Halloween Confusion

LONGINGS FOR SPRING

The coldness of the long Winter's grip
Is exceeded only by the still haunting
Of my aloneness.
How long will my season of isolation last?
How long must I endure the blasts
Of Winter's hold on me?
Where is my Springtime?
Oh, where is my time of warm release?

Come to me my season of Spring.
Bring to me your smiling rays of sunshine.
Let me hold you;
Let me bask in your ambiance;
Let me smell your sweet fragrance
As you pass by.
I long to taste the fruit of your womb;
To feel your body pressed hard against mine.

Pass on to me your warmth.
Let our pulse beat as one
As you melt my cold frame.
Let the freshness of your breath

Awaken in me the seeds of life
Planted in yesteryear.
Lacking your touch,
They remain buried, dormant.

Oh, my precious Springtime,
Come to me with haste
Lest I die in my longings.
Blow across my path and
Present to me your gift
Of sweet release.
Put an end
To my Winter's bitter grip!

REFLECTIONS OF MY HEART

I took some time to think today
Of things that form my life.
I thought about my time at work,
My children and my wife.
I thought of friends that mean so much
For all the things they do;
But all of that ground to a halt
When my thoughts fell on you!

To visualize your smile and hear
Your voice come on the phone,
No matter where I'm at in town,
It makes me feel at home.
To sense your sweet compassion
All wrapped up in words of love,
It's salvaged this poor wounded heart,
And I thank God above!

Your quick wit helps sharpen me
When I've been dulled by pain;
To sense the trust from both of you
Revives me once again.
My time with you refreshes me,
It's like nothing else;
When every side crushes me---
You bring back my pulse!

With gratefulness of heart
I give thanks to God each day
For bringing both of you to me
In such a special way.
I ask Him to protect you
As your days on earth you spend;
That as we go throughout our lives,
Our friendship will not end!

I ask Him to pour out on you
His love so rich and free;
I ask, if He would allow,
To send that love through me;
That He would open up your hearts
For you both to receive
From Him all the blessings
That your minds can conceive!

His strength and peace, His love and light,
To guide you on your path;
His hope to fill your heart each day,
His joy to help you laugh;
To trust Him to bring precious friends
Across your bumpy road,
Friends, like you, who graciously
Lighten others' loads.

You're worth more than Royalty
That sits upon a throne,
For you've reached out and touched a life
That felt so all alone.
Financial wealth is great
But it never can compare
With wealth of heart that comes
From demonstrating that you care.

To adequately 'say' the things
Deep within my heart
That I feel for all of you,
Mere words won't fit the part.
Just know that when you see my smile
In response to all you do,
It's just my way of saying
That I love all five of you!

SIMPLICITY

I
Do not need to
'DO';

I
Need to
'BE'.

COURAGE

There
Is no
'IF';

There
Is only
'WHEN'.

A GIFT THAT LASTS

Well, Christmas Day has come and passed.
Somehow I knew it wouldn't last.
Shopping done; presents wrapped;
Then suddenly it's 'Gift Attack'!

Papers flying every way
With kids a blur in the foray.
And in a moment, it's all done
As we collapse from being spun!

It seems sometimes my heart gets stirred
With Christmas now a commercial slur.
We need to stop and take a look
At what's recorded in 'The Book';

Rev'rently review the past,
Considering the age old facts.
Many gifts we give each year
But one was given, very dear.

From our Father, up above,
Came His precious gift of Love.
Clothed in likeness of mankind,
To earth He came. It was His time.

When just a child, so much He knew,
Including what He had to do.
To make this gift of Love complete,
His Father's will He had to seek.

And so He did for you and I.
That's why He bled; that's why He died.
Rejection's pain, He went through
But His love for me and you

Was worth the price He had to pay
So we could be with Him someday.
Christmas time, 2002:
What does it mean this year to you?

Gifts? Wrappings? Big Boy Toys?
Party hats and lots of noise?
Or will His gift of Love so dear
Cause you to celebrate all year?

Imagine this, if you will:
2003, each day a thrill,
Passing on the gift that lasts
To all that come across your path!

HALLOWEEN CONFUSION

Yes, 'tis the night of howls and screams,
The night we all call 'Halloween'.
The night when kids go door to door
Collecting candy as their chore.

But this does not make sense to me.
It seems instead, contradictory.
We teach them that it is not smart
To walk alone long after dark,

Then send them out when it turns night
While we stay home, out of sight.
All year long we tell them "No!"
'Bout taking things from those unknown,

Yet on this eve', in costumes graced,
We send them to some stranger's place.
"Trick-or-Treat" they're taught to say
When they get up that dark walkway.

In baggy clothes with stretched out sleeves
They're seldom told they must say "Please".
We urge them to go get these treats,
Then tell them that it rots their teeth!

They're told that trick-or-treating's fun,
But then we let them eat 'just one'.
We send them off to bed at last
With one more Halloween now passed,

Then spread the candy on the floor,
Testing each piece (it's our parental chore),
And on we sample through the night;
A quick lick here and there a bite!

And when the kids rise in the morn',
We watch with shame, their looks forlorn.
We make up some excusing song
'Bout why their candy's now all gone.

With pangs of guilt within our hearts
We fumble on and do our part
To raise their hopes, while wiping tears,
For Halloween, again next year!

Epilogue...

'So Long!'

'SO LONG!

Well, what does one say at a time like this
Knowing tomorrow his friends he'll miss?
A final 'good-bye' is too hard to say.
(I'd probably cry anyway.)

The things we've done and fun we've had
In former times made us glad.
Yet those same thoughts from yesteryears
Now flood my heart and eyes with tears!

I guess the last thing left to do
Is pray God's very best for you.
So with that prayer, tomorrow I'm gone,
But it's not 'good-bye',
It's for now. . .'So long!

ISBN 1412009386-3